IN

Nikki McClure

ABRAMS APPLESEED

NEW YORK

I only want to
stay in.
In my pajamas.
Inside.
In. In. In.

I'll climb in this basket

and there I will stay.

Until I make
a rocket ship
to fly away.

But I will only
fly in innerspace.

I'll pour milk in
mint tea
and put marmalade in
hot popovers,
then more marmalade in
more popovers.

I'll read books in laps.

And in the bathroom.

I only want to stay in.

Inside.

Indoors.

In.

In.

In . . .

In the rain.

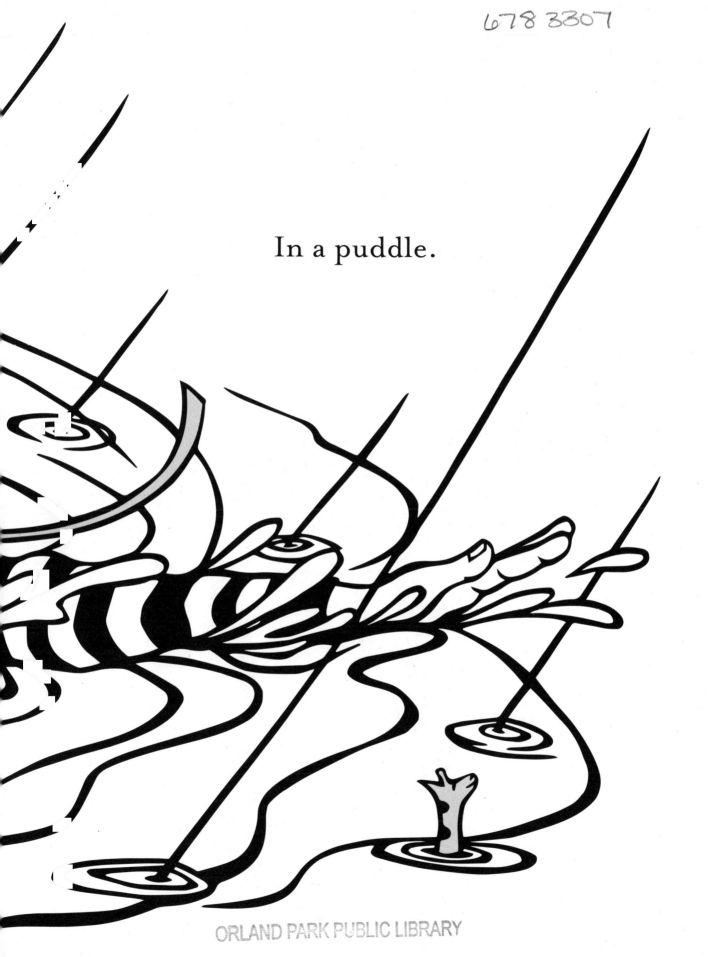

In a puddle.

Now I only want to

stay out.

Outside. Outdoors.

Out. Out. Out.

I'll look out

from branches.

Until I run out
of jam.

I'll stay out
to see an owl.

Lots of owls.

OH.

It is cold out.

It is wet out.

Now I only

want to be

in.

In my warm home.
In my bed.
In. In. In.

I really wanted to make a picture showing every kind of owl in the world, but then I learned that there are more than 200 species of owls! So I made a picture with all my *favorite* kinds of owls.

In my warm home.
In my bed.
In. In. In.

I really wanted to make a picture showing every kind of owl in the world, but then I learned that there are more than 200 species of owls! So I made a picture with all my *favorite* kinds of owls.

GUIDE

For Rowan

Cataloging-in-Publication Data has been applied for and may be obtained from the Library of Congress.

ISBN: 978-1-4197-1486-3

Text and illustrations copyright © 2015 Nikki McClure
Book design by Jessie Gang

Thank you, Susan, Steve, Scott, and KBK.

The artwork was cut from black paper using 82 X-Acto blades. The basket is one I climbed in when I was small.
The giraffe is a 10-cent garage-sale find. The yellow flag is significant.

Printed and bound in U.S.A.
10 9 8 7 6 5 4 3 2 1

For bulk discount inquiries, contact specialsales@abramsbooks.com.

ABRAMS
THE ART OF BOOKS SINCE 1949
115 West 18th Street
New York, NY 10011
www.abramsbooks.com